The Carpenters

Music Survey

By

Tony Brassington

First edition

ISBN 978-0-9569705-9-6

Published by

Tony Brassington / Mind and Achievement Ltd.

FE.V2.3

www.tonybrassington.com

Disclaimer

The book and its contents are for entertainment purposes only, and there is no attempt to claim, state, or establish absolute facts of any kind.

All responses to *The Carpenters Music Survey* represent the opinions of the people who took part in the survey and are not necessarily the opinions of the author.

Book cover design

Anisha Umělec

Original front cover watercolour artwork

Irina Bibik-Chkolian

Original back cover watercolour artwork

Mary Janzyl Elix

"Great Music Lives Forever"

Tony Brassington

Contents

Introduction

In 2017, I wrote my first Carpenters book, *The Carpenters – My Reflections*. At the time of writing that book, I thought it would be just a one-off book for me. I had no intentions to write another Carpenters book, and so I settled down to write the first two titles in my 'The Well-Travelled Book' Series: *The Avebury Ring* and *The Greatest Fortune Teller in the World.*

To my surprise, as time passed, I began to get several interesting and original ideas for writing a number of new books about the Carpenters - interesting and original are qualities I try very hard to achieve in every book I write. I knew from the interest I received from *The Carpenters – My Reflections*, and from talking to many Carpenters fans since writing it, there seemed to be a need for more books about the Carpenters. I believe *The Carpenters Music Survey* may help meet that need.

I think you will really enjoy reading this book based upon the findings of *The Carpenters Music Survey,* held in the Carpenters fiftieth-anniversary year. One hundred and fifty people took part between the 5th of August 2019 to the 29th of August 2019. They answered twenty-six questions, which took an average time of approximately thirteen minutes to complete. Many people told me they very much enjoyed taking part in the survey and found the questions to be thought-provoking and engaging.

Although only one hundred and fifty people took part, they were very carefully chosen. This survey was completed by people from all over the world, and by a number of people who actually met or knew Richard and Karen Carpenter in some way. In a few cases, possibly very well.

I sorted out, where I could, people who have been Carpenters fans for a very long time and people who understand and fully appreciate the Carpenters music in every way.

A good number of Carpenters tribute acts and some of their musicians also took part in this survey. These are people who work professionally with the Carpenters music as their day job and have a greater understanding and appreciation of everything Richard and Karen did together. (Incidentally, there were several non-tribute act drummers who took part in this survey, too.)

Questions like Q6: *Do you have a favourite Carpenters album? If so, which one?* And Q7: *Do you have a favourite album cover artwork? If so, which album?* and many others like them, reached clear conclusions that I think you will find to be quite insightful.

Some questions in the survey were multiple choices, while most others invited a written response. Where a written response was asked for, I asked questions in a way that would not try to limit the answer given to the question in any way so as to lead to more interesting and diverse responses, which it did. As a consequence, a few responses did go off topic a bit, but overall, the end result was well worth it, even though it took me some extra time to sort it all out afterwards.

Responses to survey questions

I have tried to be as accurate as possible when interpreting the data from the completed surveys. My original plan was to present the survey results by listing every response to every question, but as I began to do this, it very soon became clear that was not going to work, for a number of reasons.

In the end, I chose to present the findings from the survey in the way that I did, because I believe this format offers a more uniform and consistent tidiness in the delivery of the data from the survey.

Thanks

I would like to thank everyone that took part in *The Carpenters Music Survey.* I read every completed survey as they came in each day from all over the world, and always eagerly awaited the next one. I could not have written this book without the help and openness of all those who took part. The end result is a book that I hope you are certain to enjoy reading.

Oh, one last thing and just for fun, please say out loud, "Hello, Richard Carpenter!" because he must want to know the results of this survey too. I am sure he appreciated that as he begins reading this book.

"Those old melodies
Still sound so good to me
As they melt the years away"

'Yesterday Once More'
Written by Richard Carpenter & John Bettis)

Q1. What is your gender?

Answered: 148 Skipped: 2

Multiple choices question

Male	104 responses	70.27%
Female	41 responses	27.70%
I would prefer not to say	3 responses	2.03%

Summary

The survey begins with a very basic question, and gives a very clear answer to that question. Broadly speaking, two-thirds of those who took part in this survey were male, and one-third were female. This did surprise me a little, at first, because I imagined when I wrote the survey that the male and female mix would have been closer.

Let's speculate this for a moment. What might be the reason for these results? Whilst music can be equally enjoyed by both sexes, maybe we all have an unconscious bias towards lead singers whose songs seem to be directed to us personally. Or at least, I would imagine for most people that is how it feels.

Maybe it means that males really enjoy taking part in music surveys. Or maybe it just simply means that, on this occasion, more males than females took part in this survey.

Q2. What age are you?

Answered: 149 Skipped: 1

Multiple choices question

Under 18	1 response	0.67%
18-24	8 responses	5.37%
25–34	6 responses	4.03%
35-44	13 responses	8.72%
45-54	29 responses	19.46%
55-64	79 responses	53.02%
65+	13 responses	8.72%

Summary

On the surface of it all, the age-ranges and percentages speak for themselves, but there again, if you were to add up the first four responses from under 18 to 44, the percentage for this new group would be 18.79%, which would loosely mean that almost 20% of all those that took part were under 44 years of age. So, who says the young don't listen to the Carpenters?

Q3. How long have you enjoyed listening to the Carpenters?

Answered: 149 Skipped: 1

Multiple choices question

Less than ten years	11 responses	7.38%
More than ten years	6 responses	4.03%
More than twenty years	15 responses	10.07%
More than thirty years	14 responses	9.40%
More than forty years	103 responses	69.13%

Summary

It is quite interesting to see that eleven responses ticked the box in the survey for *listening to the Carpenters for less than ten years*, because clearly the Carpenters do not enjoy the same amount of airplay on the radio today as they did when their Singles were climbing their way up the pop charts at the peak of their careers.

I believe the one hundred and three responses that have enjoyed listening to the Carpenters for *more than forty years* provides a strong testament to the fact that the Carpenters made music that people could enjoy listening to decade after decade, throughout all the ups and downs in life and the ever-changing music scene.

Q4. Which formats do you use to listen to Carpenters music?

Answered: 147 Skipped: 3

Multiple choices question

Records / LP / 45's	64 responses	43.54%
Cassette Tapes	19 responses	12.93%
CD's / Compact Disc	117 responses	79.59%
Digital Device	105 responses	71.43%
Other	12 responses	8.16%
N/A (Not applicable)	0 responses	0.00%

(Note – Many people ticked more than one box)

Summary

It is interesting to see that Records and Cassette Tapes still have a strong following, but the world is changing, and so that must be why CD's and Digital Devices are leading the field.

Q5. How many studio albums do you think the Carpenters made together?

Answered: 147 Skipped: 2

Multiple choices question

1 to 5 Albums	0 responses	0.00%
6 to 10 Albums	55 responses	37.41%
11 or more Albums	92 responses	62.59%

Summary

My intention with this question was to see how well people know the Carpenters albums, and I was glad to see that nobody chose the response of 1 to 5 albums.

Some people might rightly argue that the answer to Q5 is not as straight forward as it might first appear.

Up to Karen's death in 1983, the Carpenters had released the following studio albums together: *Offering / Ticket To Ride, Close To You, Carpenters, A Song For You, Now & Then, Horizon, A Kind Of A Hush, Passage,* and *Made In America,* which clearly adds up to nine studio albums. In this same time period, they also released *Christmas Portrait*, an album many people may regard as a studio album. Now we are at ten, but let's not forget their phenomenally successful album, *The Singles 1969 – 1973.*

While it may well be a collection of hit singles, a number of tracks were rerecorded for this particular album, and three tracks were blended together (*Superstar, Rainy Days And Mondays*, and *Goodbye To Love*) to make one long, powerful ballad. A great deal of care was taken over producing this hit singles album, which resulted in it becoming one of the bestselling albums of the 70's. The success of *The Singles 1969 – 1973* then led to a follow up album, *The Singles 1974 – 1978*.

Richard and Karen also made a number of live albums together. Clearly these are not studio albums, but they still mean a great deal to many people.

Before Karen's death, work had begun on *Voice Of The Heart*, and this too is a very special album for many Carpenters fans.

Sometime after Karen's death, we got two more distinct albums, *Lovelines* and *As Time Goes By*. These might not be strictly studio albums that they made together, but I am sure many people do not see it that way.

That said, I think we need to allow for a generous interpretation of Q5, meaning that everyone technically gave a right answer to it, provided that nobody chose the response of 1 to 5 albums.

Q6. Do you have a favourite Carpenters album? If so, which one?

Answered: 141 Skipped: 9

No or none   3 responses

Can't choose   9 responses

All of them   3 responses

Multiple responses

Two people had more than one choice of favourite album, and these multiple answer responses have been included in the final count for each album.

Albums only chosen once (or unclear)
The Singles

Carpenters Gold

As Time Goes By

Greatest Hits

London Philharmonic

Greatest Carpenters Hits

Chosen more than once responses

Karen Carpenter (solo album)   2 responses

The Carpenters Music Survey	Tony Brassington
Ticket To Ride	2 responses
Lovelines	3 responses
Made In America	3 responses
Yesterday Once More	3 responses
A Kind Of A Hush	3 responses
Singles 1969-1973	5 responses
Voice Of The Heart	5 responses
Christmas Portrait	5 responses
Now & Then	8 responses
Carpenters (Tan album)	10 responses
Close To You	13 responses
A Song For You	29 responses
Horizon	31 responses

Summary

A Song For You and *Horizon* were the most chosen albums, and by some distance, too.

Q7. Do you have a favourite album cover artwork? If so, which album?

Answered: 141 Skipped: 9

No favourite, or like them all   19 responses

Multiple responses

Three people had more than one favourite album cover artwork, and these multiple answer responses have been included in the final count for each album.

Only chosen once responses (or unclear)

A Song For You

'The album from 1974'

Classic Carpenters

Live At The Palladium

Chosen more than once responses

Carpenters	2 responses
The Singles 1969-1973	2 responses
As Time Goes By	3 responses
Ticket To Ride / Offering	4 responses
Close To You	4 responses

Lovelines	4 responses
Voice Of The Heart	5 responses
There's A Kind Of A Hush	6 responses
Christmas Portrait	6 responses
Made In America	6 responses
Passage	11 responses
Now & Then	20 responses
Horizon	48 responses

Summary

The *Horizon* album cover received the most responses. I think it shows just how much the Carpenters were on top of their game when they made *Horizon*, with both favourite album and favourite album cover receiving the highest number of responses.

Q8. Do you think the music of the Carpenters will continue to stand the test of time?

Answered: 148 Skipped: 2

Multiple choices question

Yes	142 responses	95.95%
No	0 responses	0%
Maybe	6 responses	4.05%

Summary

The responses to Q8 gave an overwhelming Yes at almost 96%. What more can you say?

Q9. Do you like ... ?

Answered: 149 Skipped: 1

Multiple choices question

Some of their songs	3 responses	2.01%
Most of them	22 responses	14.77%
Nearly all of them	88 responses	59.06%
I like every song they sang	36 responses	24.16%

Summary

I feel these responses are very honest. The Carpenters recorded a wide range of music together. Pleasing everyone all of the time is usually nearly impossible in any area of life.

Q10. How many Carpenters albums do you own?

Answered: 149 Skipped: 1

Multiple choices question

None	7 responses	4.70%
1 to 5	19 responses	12.75%
6 to 10	19 responses	12.75%
11 or more	104 responses	69.80%

Summary

Clearly the responses to this question are saying that if you truly like the Carpenters music, then you buy as many albums as you can.

Q11. Do you have an absolute favourite Carpenters song? If so, which song?

Answered: 144 Skipped: 6

No favourite, or cannot choose   10 survey responses

Multiple responses

Eight people had more than one favourite song choice (as many as five in some responses), and these multiple answer responses have been included in the final count for each song.

Only chosen once responses (or unclear)

Sometimes

Little Alter Boy

Where Do I Go From Here?

Love Is Surrender

Guess I Just Lost My Head (Karen solo album)

And When He Smiles

Trying To Get The Feeling Again

A Place To Hideaway

Help

Maybe It's You

You Are The One

For All We Know

Ordinary Fool

I Can't Make Music

Touch Me When We're Dancing

Let Me Be The One

Reason To Believe

Sing

Two Sides

All You Get From Love Is A Love Song

When You've Got What It Takes

Kiss Me The Way You Did Last Night

Happy

Hurting Each Other

I Kept On Loving You

My Body Keeps Changing My Mind (Karen solo album)

I Believe You

Those Good Old Dreams

Chosen more than once responses

Crescent Noon   2 responses

Now	2 responses
I Won't Last A Day Without You	2 responses
One More Time	2 responses
When It's Gone	2 responses
Make Believe It's Your First Time	2 responses
You	2 responses
Ordinary Fool	2 responses
Merry Christmas Darling	3 responses
Solitaire	3 responses
For All We Know	3 responses
Superstar	3 responses
Close To You	3 responses
This Masquerade	4 responses
We've Only Just Begun	5 responses
Top Of The World	6 responses
Only Yesterday	7 responses
I Need To Be In Love	8 responses
Yesterday Once More	8 responses
Only Yesterday	9 responses
A Song For You	10 responses
Goodbye To Love	13 responses
Rainy Days And Mondays	13 responses

Summary

Q11 is a very interesting question, and there were many excellent choices for favourite song in the responses, but in the end, there were two clear winners: 'Goodbye To Love' and 'Rainy Days And Mondays'. Those two songs are very powerful and emotional. You would almost imagine 'Superstar' to be alongside them at the top; it is certainly a good fit with them.

Q12. Which Carpenters song do you feel is a hidden gem that more people should know about?

Answered: 143 Skipped: 7

No or cannot choose   5 survey responses

Multiple responses

Eight people had more than one choice of hidden gem, and these multiple answer responses have been included in the final count for each hidden gem.

Only chosen once responses

It's Really You

At The End Of A Song

Bacharach Medley

Crystal Lullaby

Sometimes

I Have You

Reason To Believe

Baby, It's You

Santa Claus Is Coming To Town

Invocation

Little Girl Blue

On The Balcony Of The Casa Rosada / Don't Cry For Me Argentina

Piano Picker

Help

Bless The Beasts And The Children

Top Of The world

A Kind Of Hush

Make Believe It's Your First Time

Two Sides

Nowadays Clancy Can't Even Sing

Rainbow Connection

I Believe You

Made In America

Ave Maria

Heather

Superstar

Lovelines

All I Can Do

What You Doing New Year's Eve

Honolulu City Lights

(A Place To) Hideaway

Eve

Sing

Where Do I Go From Here?

Only Yesterday

Chosen more than once responses

Goodbye To Love	2 responses
I Can't Make Music	2 responses
Sweet Sweet Smile	2 responses
I Just Fall In Love Again	2 responses
One Love	2 responses
Desperado	2 responses
Crescent Noon	2 responses
California Dreaming (Demo)	2 responses
Someday	2 responses
Let Me Be The One	2 responses
Kiss Me The Way You Did Last Night	2 responses
All Of My Life	2 responses
Another Song	2 responses
The Uninvited Guest	2 responses
If I Had You	2 responses
I Just Fall In Love Again	2 responses

I Believe You	2 responses
I Know I Need To Be In Love	2 responses
Leave Yesterday Behind	2 responses
B'Wana She No Home	2 responses
Solitaire	3 responses
Boat To Sail	3 responses
When It's Gone	3 responses
A Song For You	3 responses
I Can't Make Music	3 responses
I Can Dream, Can't I?	3 responses
I'm Caught Between Goodbye And I Love You	3 responses
When It's Gone	3 responses
Someday	4 responses
Happy	4 responses
Now	4 responses
Maybe It's You	4 responses
You're The One	5 responses
This Masquerade	5 responses
Trying To Get The Feeling Again	6 responses
Ordinary Fool	6 responses
You	6 responses

One More Time   7 responses

Road Ode   8 responses

Summary

This is an interesting list, and there are certainly a lot of hidden gems to choose from. When reading through the responses, if you see a song that you do not know, then that song may probably be a hidden gem well-worth looking into for you.

It is a good idea to reread this list a few times. After all, is not a hidden gem just that - hidden away in plain sight, yet still hard to find?

Q13. Do you have a favourite vocal section in a Carpenters song? (A part of a song that you love the way Karen or Richard sings the lines.)

Answered: 134 Skipped: 16

No favourite   9 responses

Like everything they sang   18 responses

Only chosen once responses

Christmas Song

Jambalaya

Ordinary Fool

Sing

The 50's Medley

I Can't Make Music

Don't Cry For Me Argentina

Reason To Believe

Maybe It's You

If I Had You

Now

Happy

Have Yourself A Merry Little Christmas

Sweet Sweet Smile

Remember When Lovin' Took All Night

You

One Love

Desperado

Calling Occupants Of Interplanetary Craft

(I'm Caught Between) Goodbye And I Love You

Christmas Portrait

Won't Last A Day Without You

Chosen more than once responses

A Song For You   2 responses

Without A Song   2 responses

Solitaire   2 responses

Love Me For What I Am	2 responses
Ave Maria	2 responses
Mr. Guder	2 responses
For All We Know	2 responses
Let Me Be The One	2 responses
We've Only Just Begun	2 responses
Ticket To Ride	2 responses
The Bacharach Medley	2 responses
Rainbow Connection	2 responses
I'll Never Fall In Love	2 responses
Close To You	2 responses
Please Mr. Postman	3 responses
Here To Remind You	3 responses
Hurting Each Other	3 responses
Rainy Days And Mondays	3 responses
Road Ode	3 responses
Merry Christmas Darling	3 responses
I Need To Be In Love	3 responses

Another Song	4 responses
Top Of The World	4 responses
Yesterday Once More	4 responses
Crescent Noon	5 responses
Superstar	5 responses
Goodbye To Love	5 responses
Only Yesterday	9 responses

Summary

Many people simply named a Carpenters song in response to Q13, and quite a number of people also included in their responses a sample of lyrics from the song, or gave some other detail as to why they thought the song was vocally special, such as what they liked about the song intro, the chorus, or the ending. Most of the responses to Q13 were widely spread across the Carpenters music catalogue, but several stood out strongly from the rest. In order to draw some meaningful conclusions from Q13, I think it is these songs we should focus on:

'Ave Maria' may have only been chosen by two people, yet both chose the entire song in their responses to Q13. Karen's rendition of 'Ave Maria' is regarded as one of the all-time best versions of this song. From the responses to other questions in this survey, that appears to be a widely-held view here also.

'Rainbow Connection' is another song where, whilst it may have received two survey responses, the responses were full of praise for the entire song. I think it is worth a mention here, because it is possibly one of their lesser known songs, but definitely not one to miss.

'Another Song' is a song that seems to engage with the listener on every level. From the opening lines of the song through the bridge melody and instrumental section, it is an invitingly rich vocal and musical feast from beginning to end.

'Top Of The World' is a song that a number of people quoted their favourite lyrics from, while others thought the whole song was excellent all the way through. It certainly is a song that perfectly flows from beginning to end; a prime example of their early work.

'Only Yesterday' was a song chosen by many, due to Karen's great phrasing of the lyrics throughout the song. Many responses also mentioned that this song has a great chorus and backing vocals.

'Crescent Noon' was loved by a number of people for its amazing vocals. The second verse and bridge were often mentioned in the responses too.

'Superstar' was chosen by five people in response to Q13. What more can be said about this well-loved song? It packs pain, hurt, feelings, and emotion into one of the most powerful ballads of all time.

'Goodbye To Love' was also chosen by five people. Karen is often admired in this song for the length of the lines she sings all in one breath.

'Only Yesterday' is the song that stands out most amongst the Q13 responses, with nine detailed responses that speak volumes about every part of this song. The responses quoted many heartfelt lyrics from the song, from beginning to end. This is a song that appears to really connect with people in a personal way.

Many of the responses to Q13 quoted the lyrics from the fourth verse of the song -

I have found my home here in your arms
Nowhere else on earth I'd really rather be
Life waits for us, share it with me
The best is about to be
And so much is left for us to see
When I hold you

(Written by John Bettis & Richard Carpenter)

As we all know, there is a great video to this song also.

Q14. Do you have a favourite Carpenters medley?

Answered: 138 Skipped: 12

In the responses to this question, some medleys were provided or known by more than one name, and there were a number of live and TV recordings also referred to, but despite the small challenge of sorting out all the individual responses, I believe the lists below are generally accurate.

Multiple responses

Some people had more than one choice of favoured medley, and these multiple answer responses have been included in the final count.

No   12 responses

Like all of them or cannot choose   11 responses

Only chosen once responses (or unclear)

Medley with Carol Burnett on YouTube

"Silly Love Songs" with Ben Vereen and the Captain and Tennille

Superstar/Rainy Days And Mondays

Top Of The World.

Las Vegas 74 Medley

Chosen more than once responses

Perry Como Medley	3 responses
Christmas Album Medley	3 responses
Close Encounters / Star Wars Medley	3 responses
London Palladium Medley	5 responses
Ella Fitzgerald Medley	7 responses
1980 TV Special/Music Music Music Medley	10 responses
Yesterday Once More/Now & Then/Oldies	39 responses
Bacharach Medley	46 responses

Summary

Q14 was a very popular question, which also proved just how well so many people love and know their Carpenters medleys.

Carol Burnett - The list of medleys begins with a real hidden gem. This is a five-minute recording taken from a Carol Burnett TV show and it is well-worth checking out if you have never seen it before.

"Silly Love Songs" with Ben Vereen and the Captain and Tennille - This too can be found on YouTube, or elsewhere on the internet. It is only about two minutes long, but it is very entertaining, and features the great vocals from all three singers.

Perry Como Medley - Perry was truly one of the greats, and so listening to him sing with the Carpenters is always a treat for the ears. This medley comes from the 1974 *Perry Como's Christmas*

Show. When watching the video, it shows in their eyes how much they all appear to enjoy singing together, and how much they feel the music too. This medley is five minutes of pure awesomeness.

Christmas Album Medley - Carpenters Christmas albums remain as popular as ever. They contain so much great music, including first-class medleys of Christmas songs.

Ella Fitzgerald Medley - this medley shows two remarkable singers giving a wonderful performance together. It includes a superior duet section from these two great singers.

1980 TV Special/Music Music Music Medley - ten minutes of great music and vocals covering a wide spectrum of the Carpenters' music, which is always a treat to listen to. There is a video to this medley, which is awesome to watch, too.

Now & Then/Yesterday Once More Medley - this medley received thirty-five responses (loosely speaking, 25% of all the responses to Q14). I have always considered this medley to be the most fun of all. It is truly an evergreen medley that never tires.

Bacharach Medley - this medley received the most responses at forty-three (loosely speaking, 31% of all the responses to Q14). This medley can be found on *Carpenters* 1971 Tan album, and clearly contains so many well-loved classic songs.

Q15. Is there a Carpenters song that means a lot to you personally?

Answered: 139 Skipped: 11

Multiple responses

Some people had more than one choice of song, so these multiple answer responses have been included in the final count.

No   12 responses

Yes, or many   9 responses

Only chosen once responses

At The End Of A Song

Sweet, Sweet Smile

All You Get From Love Is A Love Song

Desperado

Help

I Believe You

I Have You

I Just Fall In Love Again

For All We Know

Merry Christmas Darling

One More Time

Sing

Tryin' To Get The Feeling Again

They Long To Be Close To You

You

Your Baby Doesn't Love You Anymore

Because We Are In Love (The Wedding Song)

Chosen more than once responses

Road Ode   2 responses

Make Believe It's Your First Time   2 responses

Maybe It's You   2 responses

I Can't Make Music   2 responses

I'm Caught Between Goodbye & I Love You   2 responses

Happy   2 responses

Look To Your Dreams   2 responses

The Carpenters Music Survey	Tony Brassington
Love Me For What I Am	2 responses
I Won't Last A Day Without You	3 responses
Close To You	3 responses
Goodbye To Love	4 responses
Solitaire	4 responses
Superstar	4 responses
Sometimes	5 responses
Top Of The World	6 responses
Only Yesterday	7 responses
Now	7 responses
A Song For You	7 responses
Yesterday Once More	7 responses
Rainy Days And Monday	9 responses
I Need To Be In Love	10 responses
We've Only Just Begun	12 responses

Summary

Most of the responses to Q15 simply named a song that meant a lot to them personally, but did not go into details, which is quite understandable when the question is a personal topic. From those that did write a few words in response to Q15, I have added a few highlights.

Many people chose a Carpenters song they can clearly remember as being the first one they ever heard and, in most cases, was a childhood memory. Interestingly, apart from one response, all the rest of the songs in this category were songs prior to 1974; such as 'We've Only Just Begun', 'Yesterday Once More', 'Sing', 'Top Of The World', and 'Close To You' - the kind of songs which many years ago would have had a lot of radio airtime.

One response provided an interesting story about hearing 'Close To You' for the first time. There was a Korean TV show called *She Was Pretty,* and 'Close To You' was played on it. From that point on, this person fell in love with Karen's voice and the music that Richard arranged so beautifully.

'A Song For You', one person wrote that they have requested this song for their funeral as it always feels like Karen is singing just to them. Karen does indeed have that special quality of making you feel she's singing just to you.

'Only Yesterday' was chosen in one response because that person met Karen on five occasions the same year the song was climbing the pop charts.

'Sometimes' was given praise by one responder to Q15 who said that for the last sixteen years, the words of this song have been an important part of a collage under a clear sheet of Plexiglass on this person's desk to serve as a daily reminder of the things that matter most in life. As songs go, there are relatively few lyrics, but they are very significant and meaningful.

Sometimes, not often enough

We reflect upon the good things

And those thoughts always centre

Around those we love

And I think about those people

Who mean so much to me

And for so many years have made me

So very happy

And I count the times I have forgotten to say

Thank you, and just how much I love them

(Written by Felice Mancini)

Q16. Are there any lyrics from a Carpenters song that really resonate with you personally, or make you feel quite emotional?

Answered: 137 Skipped: 13

Multiple responses

Some people had more than one choice of song lyrics, so these multiple answer responses have been included in the final count.

No   12 responses

Like all of them or cannot choose   8 responses

Only chosen once responses

Aurora

Eventide

(A Place To) Hideaway

Won't Last A Day Without You

Make Believe It's Your First Time

Love Me For What I Am

Road Ode

Rainbow Connection

You're The One

Happy

Slow Dance

Where Do I Go From Here

Trying To Get The Feeling

Crystal Lullaby

One More Time

This Masquerade

I Believe You

Sandy

All Of My Life

Let Me Be The One

Crescent Noon

Chosen more than once responses

When It's Gone	2 responses
For All We Know	2 responses
Maybe It's You	2 responses
I'm Caught Between Goodbye And I Love You	2 responses
You	2 responses
When You Have Got What It Takes	2 responses
Superstar	2 responses
We've Only Just Begun	2 responses

The Carpenters Music Survey   Tony Brassington

I Can't Make Music	3 responses
Close To You	3 responses
Sometimes	3 responses
Look To Your Dreams	3 responses
Top Of The World	3 responses
One Love	4 responses
Merry Christmas Darling	4 responses
Only Yesterday	4 responses
Solitaire	5 responses
Goodbye To Love	6 responses
Rainy Days And Mondays	6 responses
Yesterday Once More	8 responses
Now	10 responses
A Song For You	12 responses
I Need To Be In Love	19 responses

Summary

The responses to Q16 were a fairly even mix of just the name of a Carpenters song or the name of a song with an example of lyrics from that song. A few responses had an example of lyrics only, and there were a great many comments too, throughout all of the responses, relative to the personal significance of certain songs and lyrics. I think the responses to Q16 show just how much the Carpenters songs still connect with people.

'Aurora and Eventide' are both very short songs that come from the *Horizon* album. 'Aurora' is at the beginning of the album, and 'Eventide' is at the end. One person named both of these songs in their response and said that they generate a lot of emotion for them. When you listen to the lyrics, these two songs do capture something very special with the combination of Karen's voice and Richards's arrangement; they are certainly two very unique songs.

'Road Ode' one person quoted the lyrics from, because it always reminded that person of being on the road alot many years ago, driving on some pretty, quiet highways in the Midwest.

'Sandy', a lovely song from *A Kind Of A Hush*, one person wrote about their dog and how they did have time to chase the winter away together.

'Look To Your Dreams' received a lot of praise for the inspiring motivational lyrics to be found throughout the song.

'Only Yesterday' had many of the lyrics quoted in the responses to this great Carpenters love song.

'Yesterday Once More' had nearly all of the responses quote only the song title, which I assume means that they like the lyrics of the song all the way through.

'Now' had a similar response as the prior song, where the majority of the responses quoted only the song title.

'A Song For You' clearly means a lot to many people. These lyrics were often included in the responses to Q16.

And when my life is over
Remember when we were together.
We were alone, and I was singing this song for you.
(Written by Leon Russell)

Many people said that Karen's rendition of this song has such a personal feel about it and it really does feel as if Karen is singing just to them. That level of vocal performance is quite something.

'I Need To Be In Love' is believed to have been Karen's favourite Carpenters song. I am sure she would have been pleased to see it come out on top in Q16 with nineteen responses. Around half of the responses that chose 'I Need To Be In Love' quoted heart-felt lyrics from across the whole song. I get the impression that many people can truly relate to the lyrics of the song through their own life experience. 'I Need To Be In Love' is a song that truly connects with people.

Q17. Is there a song that the Carpenters never sang, but you wish that they had?

Answered: 135 Skipped: 15

Note - I found when analysing all of the responses to Q17, they came with a few extra challenges. The responses were mostly a song title or a song title with an artist name. I determined for the most part to keep as close as possible to the original responses, because many songs have a long history and many have been performed by a number of artists over the years, and there's more than one song by the same song title, in some cases. So, for those reasons, I did not add an artist name where one was not already given in response to Q17.

(Not every response to Q17 is included.)

No or cannot choose   35 responses

Only chosen once responses

I Can't Help Falling In Love With You

Delilah

But Not For Me

Ev'ry Time We Say Goodbye

You Belong To Me

At Seventeen

I Honestly Love You

The First Time Ever I Saw Your Face

Light My Fire

The Wind Beneath My Wings

Rock With You

Way Back Into Love

River Deep, Mountain High

Show Me The Way To Your Heart

Que Sera Sera

It Never Rains In Southern California

I Hear Those Church Bells Ringing

Killing Me Softly With His Song

Through The Years

You Don't Have To Say You Love Me.

Day Dream Believer

Fields Of Gold

Everything

You've Got A Friend

Tracks Of My Tears

You Are My Sunshine

You're My World

I Wish I Didn't Love You So

I Can't Make You Love Me

Nobody Does It Better

How Can I Be Sure

Broken Hearted Me

When You Wish A Upon A Star

I'm So Lonesome I Could Cry.

I Say A Little Prayer

Pure Imagination

What's New (by Linda Ronstadt)

Same Ole Love (by Anita Baker)

Secret Love (by Doris Day)

Home (by Michael Buble)

Now and Forever (by Anne Murray)

Until It's Time For You To Go (by Nancy Sinatra)

In The Wee Small Hours Of The Morning (by Frank Sinatra)

Can't Help Falling In Love (by Elvis)

Mornin (by Al Jarreau)

Don't Answer Me (by the Alan Parsons Project)

Eye In The Sky (by the Alan Parsons Project)

This Used To Be My Playground (by Madonna)

Crazy For You (by Madonna)

You've Got A Friend (by Carole King)

It's Too Late (by Carole King)

White Flag (by Dido)

Life For Rent (by Dido)

Here With Me (by Dido)

Name Of The Game (by Abba)

Thank You For The Music (by Abba)

Yesterday (by The Beatles)

Something (by The Beatles)

Hey Jude (by The Beatles)

Surfs Up (by The Beach Boys)

In My Room (by The Beach Boys)

"Any Beach Boys tune"

Little Christmas Tree

Christmas List

Hopelessly Devoted To You (from the film *Grease*)

Where Do I Begin? (Movie theme from *Love Story)*

Chosen more than once responses

Somewhere Over The Rainbow	2 responses
We're All Alone (by Rita Coolidge)	2 responses
Star Spangled Banner	2 responses
Memory (from the musical *Cats*)	2 responses
Oh Holy Night	4 responses
The Way We Were	4 responses

The following include responses for songs that have in some way already (in full or in part) been sung or recorded by the Carpenters.

Funny Valentine (part of the medley with Ella Fitzgerald)

Tony Brassington

A House Is Not A Home (part of the medley "Make Your Own Kind of Music" TV special in 1971.)   2 responses

Something In Your Eyes (Time album)   3 responses

It's Impossible (Part of the Perry Como medley) 3 responses

Summary

Reading through the responses to Q17, I found many interesting ideas amongst them. As I read them all, I tried to imagine Karen singing some of them. It was easy to see how many of those songs would have suited her amazing voice.

One that stood out for me was 'Pure Imagination'. I believe it was first sung by Gene Wilder in the film *Willy Wonka & the Chocolate Factory* (1971) - quite an intriguing choice. It is a song that unfolds slowly, and I think it would have suited Karen's style and phrasing perfectly. Add to that Richard Carpenter's arrangement, it would have worked very well.

'Broken Hearted Me' (Anne Murray, 1970) I thought was another good choice.

'Killing Me Softly' by Roberta Flack (1972) - Oh wow, can you just imagine feeling the pain and emotion if Karen had sung that song? It would have been right up there with 'Goodbye To Love', 'Rainy Days And Mondays', and 'Superstar'.

In truth, Q17 is a fascinating read, full of so many interesting song choices to ponder what might have been. Ultimately, I think there is no right or wrong answer as it is a personal choice.

Q18. How would you describe Karen's voice?

Answered: 142 Skipped: 8

The responses to this question were quite interesting to review. A few describe Karen's voice from a purely technical understanding of singing; some describe her voice from the point of view of how it makes the listener feel and their appreciation of it, while many others use comparative words and terminology.

Amongst the comparative words and terminology, we find many very apt words used to describe Karen's voice, such as:

natural
angelic
voice of an angel
not of this world
gift from God
heaven sent
other worldly
as of the sound of God
velvet
velvet voice
liquid velvet
pure velvet
pure
soothing
smooth
smooth as silk
silky honey
beautiful
beautifully silky
syrup and honey

intimate
heartfelt
exquisite
perfection
absolute perfection
unique
magical
warm
friendly
personal
emotional
sensual
rich
affecting
tender
one-of-a-kind
sweet
sophisticated
timeless
flawless
pitch perfect
depth of feeling
raw
technically brilliant
depth of feeling
phenomenal
expressive
controlled
precise

These words came up time and time again in response to Q18. For so many people, Karen's voice was all of those things and so much more.

Amongst the responses that described Karen's voice from the point of view of how it makes them feel, or their appreciation of it, there were many comments such as:

'Karen's voice draws the listener in like no other singer can.'
'The best voice in the business.'
'The best female voice ever.'
'The most beautiful sound I have ever heard.'
'Karen's voice goes right to my heart.'
'Warm and comforting.'
'Like melted chocolate.'
'A kiss to the eardrums.'

A number of responses mentioned how Karen's voice felt like it could reach inside a person and touch their very soul. When you think about it, perhaps that is the greatest thing for any singer to aspire for and ultimately hope to achieve!

Summary

How can you begin to describe Karen's voice in a way that could really do it justice? While it's true there are many good singers out there, and a few great ones too, Karen's voice is in a league all on its own. The more you listen to her sing, the more you appreciate just how special she was - a total one-off, unreplaceable.

Q19. Which Carpenters song do you feel demonstrates Karen's vocal talents the most?

Answered: 139 Skipped: 11

Don't know or cannot choose   10 Responses

Only chosen once responses

Reason To Believe

End Of The World

Merry Christmas Darling

Guess I Just Lost My Head

Santa Claus Is Coming To Town

Christ Is Born

I'll Be Home For Xmas

For All We Know

Sleigh Ride

Da Doo Ron

Ordinary Fool

Two Sides

I Can't Make Music

Eve

Let Me Be The One

Now

When He Smiles.

I'm Caught Between Goodbye And I love You

Chosen more than once responses

Another Song	2 responses
Little Altar Boy	2 responses
If I Had You	2 responses
You're The One	2 responses
I Can Dream Can't I	2 responses
Top Of The world	2 responses
Desperado	2 responses
Have Yourself A Merry Little Christmas	3 responses
Don't Cry For Me Argentina	3 responses
We've Only Just Begun	4 responses

The Carpenters Music Survey	Tony Brassington
Crescent Noon	4 responses
Close To You	4 responses
Yesterday Once More	4 responses
Rainy Days And Mondays	4 responses
I Need To Be In Love	5 responses
This Masquerade	5 responses
Only Yesterday	6 responses
Goodbye To Love	9 responses
A Song For You	9 responses
Ave Maria	12 responses
Superstar	13 responses
Solitaire	25 responses

Summary

The three most chosen responses were 'Solitaire' from the album *Horizon,* which was clearly the winner with twenty-five responses, 'Superstar' received thirteen responses, closely followed by 'Ave Maria' with twelve responses. But I think you will agree that there were many truly great candidates to showcase Karen's singing talents amongst all the other responses.

Q20. Which Carpenters song do you feel demonstrates Richard's musical talents the best?

Answered: 138 Skipped: 11

Don't know   10 responses

Can't choose, most of them, all of them   10 responses

Only chosen once responses

Santa Claus Is Comin' To Town

Iced Tea

Flat Baroque

One Love

From This Moment On

Look To Your Dreams

Now

Nowadays Clancy

Song For You.

Time

Help

When It's Gone

Calling Your Name Again

Hurting Each Other

Kiss Me

Turn Away

Walk On By

Top Of The World

You're The One

Merry Christmas Darling.

Bacharach David Medley

Carpenters Medley

Chosen more than once responses

Warsaw Concerto	2 responses
Solitaire	2 responses
Karen's Theme	2 responses
Your Wonderful Parade	2 responses

Sometimes	2 responses
Saturday	2 responses
Mr. Guder	3 responses
Heather	3 responses
Only Yesterday	4 responses
Superstar	5 responses
Yesterday Once More	6 responses
Ticket To Ride	6 responses
Goodbye To Love	6 responses
Piano Picker	7 responses
I Kept On Loving You	8 responses
Close To You	8 responses
We've Only Just Begun	8 responses
This Masquerade	9 responses
Calling Occupants Of Interplanetary Craft	11 responses

Summary

This is actually a very good question, and when you really think about it, there are many excellent examples of Richard's numerous talents. It could be argued that every Carpenters song showcases Richard's talents, and the great diversity in the responses to Q20 appears to endorse that line of thought.

'Calling Occupants Of Interplanetary Craft', not too surprisingly, received the most responses to Q20; it is truly an excellent choice.

Carpenters With the Royal Philharmonic Orchestra, *Richard Carpenter: Pianist, Arranger, Composer* and *Christmas Portrait*, were the three albums praised for Richard's work on the entire album.

Many responses included some general comments to describe Richards's musical talents, such as:

'He is very talented.'
'Pure genius'
'Unparalleled'
'All of his arrangements are superb.'
'His arrangements are generally all brilliant.'

Q21. Have you ever been to a Carpenters concert?

Answered: 148 Skipped: 2

Multiple choices Question

Yes	55 Responses	37.16%
No	93 Responses	62.84%

Q22. Have you ever been to a Carpenters tribute concert?

Answered: 149 Skipped: 1

Multiple choices Question

Yes	44 Responses	29.53%
No	105 Responses	70.47%

Summary

I decided to put Q21 & Q22 together on the same page, because they are closely related to each other. For me, it was noticeable each day as the responses came in that the percentages were virtually the same for both questions. Generally speaking, one-third had been to a Carpenters concert, or tribute act concert, and two-thirds had not. This might change in the future, because there is a growing number of truly excellent tribute acts out there.

Interestingly, when I took a closer look at all of the responses to Q21 and Q22, I found fifteen responders had been to both, which is approximately 10%.

Q23. If you had the chance to talk to Richard Carpenter, what would you like to say to him?

Answered: 141 Skipped: 9

"I'd thank him for providing the soundtrack to my life."

There were so many varied and interesting responses to Q23. For example, one person mentioned he would like to talk to Richard Carpenter about his car collection; which I imagine, if the situation arose and time would allow, would be a long conversation that they might both enjoy.

Another wanted to ask if Richard would please consider producing a few tracks with UK singer, Harriet, since *'She comes closest to duplicating the magic of Karen."*

One lady wrote that she would first say, *'Thank you!'* and then mention that the Carpenters music had been a great influence on her life and that Karen was her first vocal coach at age eight. (I'm assuming that must have been in a singalong capacity?)

A few responses said they would like to talk to Richard about the technical side of song-writing and arranging. I think a lot could be learned from a conversation like that with Richard.

A number of Carpenters tribute acts said very similar things to one another in their responses, along the lines of:

"Thank you for the music."
"You are a musical genius; please come see our tribute show."

Many responses wanted to tell Richard how much Richard's and Karen's music had been a positive influence throughout their lives (often from an early age) - an influence which brought with it a lifetime of joy and strength.

Several responses wanted to ask Richard if there were any more Carpenters music yet to be released, such as from the television shows they made, tracks that were recorded that never made it on to a Carpenters album, or Karen Carpenters solo album.

There were many responses complimenting Richard and Karen on their contributions to music and all they achieved together, as well as praises geared towards Richard on the way he's managed the Carpenters musical legacy since Karen's death. Richard's solo albums and the latest album, *The Carpenters with the Royal Philharmonic Orchestra* received many compliments, in addition to answers testifying to Richard's great music skill, knowledge and genius.

One thing stood above all in response to Q23. More than half of the people who answered this question wanted to say one thing to Richard: thank you. *'Thank you,'* and *'Thank you for the music,'* were the most common responses of this type, often combined with a personal heartfelt comment or two.

The responses to Q23 shine a light on the kind of questions that Richard must have been asked so many times before. Overall, the responses to this question show a great deal of love and respect for all that Richard has done, combined with genuine thanks and heartfelt gratitude for the enriching of peoples' lives through the Carpenters music.

Q24. If Karen Carpenter was still alive today and you had a chance to talk to her, what would you say?

Answered: 139 Skipped: 11

Q24 was the most challenging section to write up a summary for, because Q24 had the longest written responses of all, and these longer responses were quite diverse. They made several separate points within each.

Here are some random samples that throw some light on the great diversity of responses -

'Can I give you a hug?'
'I love your solo album!'
'I can't wait for your next album!'
'Let's go to Disney World.'
'When does your film career begin?'
'I've had a crush on you since the early 70's.'

Drums - Three of the responses mentioned how Karen had been a positive influence for them as a drummer, and two of the three ultimately became professional drummers.

Role model - A number of responses wanted to tell Karen that she had been very much a role model for them that allowed them to hope and dream (often from childhood), and for showing them, *"It is okay to be yourself and to express yourself without feeling that you have to hide every quirky part of your personality."*

Self-worth / Self-image - Many responses wished to express to Karen supportive things like:

'You are a beautiful person inside and out.'

'You are special just as you are.'

'Please love yourself more.'

'Respect yourself.'

'She is loved by many more then she knew (knows).'

'Why couldn't you see how talented you were?'

'Please don't suffer in silence.'

Love - Quite a number of responses talked in terms of love - some in fond admiration, while others appeared to mean it in its more direct and personal sense. They wanted to tell Karen directly that they love her. A number of people mentioned how Karen's death affected them at the time it happened, and how they still deeply feel it even now. Three responses simply said, **'Marry me.'**

Voice / singing

Common responses of things people wanted to say to Karen on this topic were along these lines:

'You have a beautiful, wonderful, absolutely amazing voice.'

'You have a God given talent with the voice of an angel.'

'Without any doubt you have one of the finest voices of all time, and the best singing voice of all time.'

'You are the greatest vocalist ever.'

'Your music touches my very soul, and you always sound like you are singing just for me; your voice is not just simply heard but felt deep in inside me also.'

Assorted Thanks

Although the actual words, *'Thanks,'* and *'Thank You,'* were only used in forty-five responses, virtually every response (around 99% of them) were warm, friendly, caring, loving, complimentary and supportive. A great many talked about Karen like she was an old friend, or as a person they felt like they had known all their life. Throughout, there was a great deal of thanks and appreciation for the wonderful music that Karen and Richard made together. It is very clear from all of the responses that Karen was a person who really touched people's lives.

Summary

As you read through this chapter of the book, it is absolutely clear just how much Karen still means to people, and how much she is still greatly missed to this very day.

Q25. Have you or a family member ever met Richard or Karen Carpenter in the past? If so, please give a brief description of it.

Answered: 130 Skipped: 20

As might be expected, most responses to Q25 could only answer *no* to this question. Out of 130, only twenty-two responses wrote about having met them in person, either separately or together. However, of those who had not met the Carpenters, there were a number of interesting responses which I have also included.

Met both of them

One guy wrote, *'I had the pleasure of working with them in the mid-70's.'* After reading through his completed survey, I would say that he knew them quite well, too.

Apart from that response, nearly all of those who had met both Richard and Karen, they met them at a concert (usually after it). The only person that met them before a concert, and did so at a rehearsal for a concert, said that he found them both to be very kind and unassuming, and still has their autographed photo today.

One responder said he received autographs from them both after the concert. He said he will always remember that Karen changed her clothes and was relaxing while eating chicken.

One guy met them in 1976 in Toronto after a concert, and another guy was lucky enough to meet them twice, once at a concert in 1972, and again in 1974.

Another person met them both late one evening after a concert in Ohio. *'They both looked tired, but agreed to sign my poster.'*

A lady wrote in her response that she met them after a concert in 1971, and Karen personally thanked her for coming to see them.

A friend of mine, who also took part in this survey, wrote in her response about the time her dad met the Carpenters:

' My dad was a WOII (Warrant Officer 2) in the Royal Marines. In 1975 Richard and Karen Carpenter were on tour in Malta and they were performing at the Dragonara Palace hotel, my dad and the rest of his soldiers / Royal Marines, watched them in concert and saw them back stage afterwards, and asked them if they would like to come back to the Sergeants mess (as my dad was an officer) for the rest of the evening to have drinks and chill out.

Karen and Richard came alone, they didn't have any bodyguards or entourage or roadies with them which made the soldiers feel very special. They had a tuneless piano in the corner and so obviously they were encouraged to sing a couple of songs, but my dad can't remember which songs, sorry.

My dad's memory of them personally was that Karen was very pleasant and easy to talk to, but Richard was a bit more difficult to talk to. Probably a case of not being able to find common ground I would imagine!'

Met Richard

There were fourteen responses that were written about meeting Richard. One spoke of attending Karen's funeral service and later that year briefly speaking to Richard during a tribute concert for Karen in June 1983. Most of the other responses were of meeting Richard at a wide range of various social events: charity concerts, Christmas concerts, Jazz festivals, Carpenters-themed events, and events relating to Richard's solo albums.

In 1983, a pianist was working at the Salt Lake Marriott. Richard and his family came in for Sunday Brunch. He was lucky enough to talk with Richard for some time afterwards.

Interesting miscellaneous responses

Although one responder stated he never actually met Richard or Karen, he wrote of his experience of being on the A&M Records soundstage a number of times in the 1970s and early 1980s, and how it still brings back fond memories for him all these years later whenever he drives past it.

Two responses wrote about meeting the Carpenters in a dream, and both said it happened more than once. The first one wrote, *'Never met them, only in the odd dream or two,'* and the second response was, *'I have dreamt that I was on their road crew several times.*

One lady shared a very personal and deeply touching story in her responses. After Karen's death, she went to visit the Forest Lawn Memorial Park to place a yellow rose in Karen's memory. She was crying her heart out at the moment when an older couple came up to her and asked her if she was alright. It took a while to figure out who the couple was, but then she realised it was Mr. & Mrs. Carpenter, Harold and Agnes. She stated she felt worse, because they were asking *her* if she was alright, understandably.

Summary

I think for most people, the biggest surprise-finding of Q25 are the accounts of people meeting the Carpenters in their dreams. When you also consider how few people could actually respond to Q25 with relative experience of actually meeting Richard and Karen Carpenter (twenty-seven altogether) in the first place, then the two responses that shared their dream experiences of meeting them actually represents not-an-insignificant percentage of all the responses to Q25. It is easy to imagine that there may have been a few more people who took part in this survey who have also had dream experiences with Karen or Richard, but who might not have wanted to share them, or even realised that they could have.

If you then extend this to the wider population, by extension, this must mean that Richard and Karen have showed up in the dreams of potentially hundreds, if not thousands, of people, perhaps? … That is quite a fascinating line of thought to ponder.

Q26. Do you think that there were any especially defining moments in the Carpenter's careers?

Answered: 128 Skipped: 22

Yes or cannot choose   7 responses

No or cannot answer   18 responses

Success in the early 1970s

There were around twenty general responses that focused on the many areas of Carpenters successes in the early 1970s, followed by a few for the early 1980s.

Quaaludes addiction   2 responses

Two responses commented on Richard's decision to seek help for his addiction to Quaaludes as a defining moment. In truth, anyone who can admit that they have an addiction problem of any kind and face up to it, has certainly reached an important moment in their life.

We've Only Just Begun   2 responses

This Carpenters song was chosen in two responses as an especially defining moment.

A Song For You   2 responses

'A Song For You' was also twice chosen as a defining moment.

Goodbye To Love   3 responses

Three survey responses chose this song as a defining moment for the Carpenters, and it does certainly have a number of standout qualities. The use of the fuzz guitar is still much talked about even now, all these years later. Also, many have recognised this song as the first ever power ballad.

Passage   3 responses

The album *Passage* was pointed out as a defining moment for the Carpenters in three responses. It is an album that is well-regarded as being very innovative and creative.

The White House   5 responses

The Carpenters playing for President Nixon at the White House; an understandably good choice for a defining moment.

Christmas Portrait   6 responses

This album and alot of the songs from it have made a very strong appearance throughout this survey. The holiday content of this album obviously sets it apart from the Carpenters main body of work; even so, it is very clear that this album is very well-loved by a great many people.

Drums   6 responses

Karen having to come out from behind the drums to take centre stage was pointed out as a defining moment in six responses. It is a joy to watch her playing the drums. She looks so happy playing them, but when you really think about it, how long could the girl with the amazing voice resist taking her rightful place on centre stage? Surely, it had to happen in the end.

TV specials   7 responses

After so many years of concert tours, television was really quite a change of direction for the two. The Carpenters TV Specials did produce plenty of good music in many forms, duets and medleys with guests, and, of course, Christmas songs too.

Horizon   7 responses

It is no surprise to see the album *Horizon* make it onto this list of defining moments. This album and many of the songs from it have had strong presence throughout this survey. As one response put it, *'This album is pure magic.'*

Grammy awards   8 responses

After their great successes in the early years, the Carpenters won three Grammys and were nominated for many more. From there, they still went on to create so much more great music.

Herb Alpert / A&M Records   9 responses

Without any doubt, signing a recording contract with Herb Alpert/ A&M Records was a very special moment in time for them. Herb Alpert pretty much let the Carpenters have free reign to do what they wanted in order to create their distinct sound. They were in exactly the right place; many other record companies might not have been so accommodating.

Karen's solo album   11 responses

The events surrounding the recording and subsequent shelving of Karen's solo album are very well-documented, and they remain controversial to this day. I think, as the years pass, it becomes increasingly difficult to remember the world as it was then, and so perhaps, we are probably not best-placed to judge the decisions made by others at the time. We can, however, now enjoy listening to Karen's solo album today, and to enjoy her solo album is surely what Karen would have wanted us all to do, without any ill will towards others.

Anorexia   11 responses

There were eleven wide-ranging responses mentioning Karen's illness - from the early stages, up to her all too-early death. As one person wrote, *"There must have been a moment Karen started feeling less than...,"* but then, who knows for sure? Karen's death was a great tragedy, which is still felt by so many all these years later.

Close To You   25 responses

Both the single and album for this were enormously successful. Without any doubt, 'Close to You' gained the most responses for the Carpenters defining moments in this survey.

Summary

Q26 provided a wide assortment of responses spread across the lives and careers of Richard and Karen Carpenter. When you think about it, there are a number of categories to subdivide Q26 by. A defining moment in the Business side of the Carpenter's careers, a defining moment in the Musical side of the Carpenter's careers, a defining moment in the personal lives of Richard and Karen. The list could possibly go on further than that. But because this is 'The Carpenters Music Survey', then *Close To You* with its twenty-five responses is probably the kind of result we were looking for.

Final comments from the author

Once again, I would like to thank everyone who took part in this survey as I could not have done it without you. I would especially like to thank all those people who were brave and honest enough to share with me what were, at times, some of their most private thoughts, feelings and experiences.

For me, it has been an absolute pleasure working on, both the original survey, and this final book. It was so enjoyable reading the completed surveys as they came in each day and equally enjoyable processing the survey data into this book.

While I was working on this book, I personally felt very happy and content within myself, and I was very excited about the content of the book. I felt the same way when I wrote *White Horses Live Forever*. And in both cases, as an author, I knew that the content of each respective book was just so right for the reader to enjoy.

As I wrote this book, I thought it was best to let you read through *The Carpenters Music Survey* with only a minimum of comments from me along the way. By doing that, the survey is allowed to truly speak for itself, and be more open to interpretation by any reader, without too much influence by my own opinion. Hopefully I have succeeded in that. Here in this final conclusion, I feel I can provide an overview of some of my own thoughts and conclusions relating to *The Carpenters Music Survey*.

It should always be remembered that this is only one survey - a snapshot of many people's thoughts, opinions, likes and dislikes at one point in time, and those that took part were widely spread across the world.

Even so, I believe that there are a number of clear findings that stand out very well, such as, for instance, the album *Horizon*. It took joint first place for people's favourite Carpenters album (Q6), and first place for favourite album cover artwork (Q7). 'Solitaire' was well in front of its rivals for the song that demonstrates Karen's vocal talents the most (Q19). After reading this book, if you do not already own a copy of *Horizon*, then now might be time to buy one, and if you do own a copy of this old favourite, then I suspect you will be playing it again very soon.

I strongly believe this survey also stands testament to how well the Carpenter's earlier songs and albums have stood the test of time. When you think about it, it is hard to imagine any new artist hitting the music scene today with songs up to the standards and quality of 'Close To You', 'Superstar', 'Rainy Days And Mondays', and 'Goodbye To Love', to name only a few. The Carpenters did truly achieve something so very special together - something that very few artists could ever hope or dream of matching. They are a shining example of perfection, both musically and vocally, and even after all these years, they remain a very hard act to follow.

I believe that this is a book that you can read many times over and always enjoy, because *The Carpenters Music Survey* is about so much more than simply just highlighting the biggest and best of all that Richard and Karen did together.

There is so much beauty to be found in the small stuff: the unique heartfelt comments, the fact that lovers of the Carpenters music even dream about them. Reading between the lines, many things are clear; for example, this survey also proves that the Carpenters Christmas albums / songs are as well-loved as many of their well-known chart hits. I think the more this survey is read, the more it actually reveals to the reader. But there is one thing that is crystal clear, *The Carpenters Music Survey* proves just how much the Carpenters are still loved, listened to, and appreciated in every way, and that is because

"Great Music Lives Forever"

Other Books by Tony Brassington

Carpenters Books by Tony Brassington –

The Carpenters - My Reflections

-In *The Carpenters- My Reflections*, I share my own personal experience of listening to the Carpenters for many decades of my life. The book also looks at the great number of changes over the years in the way we store and listen to music.

-I am currently working on my next Carpenters book, and I can promise you that book will be something quite special and unique.

The Well-Travelled Book Series – Current titles include

The Avebury Ring

The Greatest Fortune Teller In The World

White Horses Live Forever

The Well-Travelled Book Series is an interesting, entertaining, and diverse series of unrelated short stories. Because these stories are all unrelated, they can be read in any order. They all contain a mixture of fiction combined with personal development and personal growth, and many life lessons, too, while remaining true to the 'Laws of the Universe' and 'The Laws of Success.'

The Well-Travelled Book Series also encourages giving and sharing; which is something we all individually need to do more of, as well as collectively, for everyone's mutual benefit. This is done in an easy and fun way that encourages sharing, not just by you, but with subsequent readers of each well-travelled book, too. At the back of each book is a section where each Well-Travelled Book tells of its travels and adventures.

After reading it, each reader can take a pen and write in the book: their name, where in the world they were when they read it, and the date when they read it. The reader is then encouraged to give the book to another person. As the list of readers, dates, and locations grow, this section of the book will become a fascinating read, as each book tells the reader all about its well-travelled life.

This simple act of giving and sharing in this way may prove to be more helpful to you than it might first appear. We live in a world where everything has its equal opposite - one of the 'Laws of the Universe' - so when we are trying to attract our dreams and goals into our lives, we are asking to receive something. The opposite of receiving is giving. Ponder this concept for a few moments and you will begin to see the great importance of giving in order to receive.

Good stories need good characters and environments to underpin each story and bring it to life in an interesting and entertaining way. *The Well-Travelled Book* Series does well on both of those counts. All of the stories in the series are set in or around the beautiful city of Bath and surrounding areas. This part of England is rich with history, both ancient and modern, allowing the stories in *The Well-Travelled Book* series to visit ancient stone circles and an assortment of other unique ancient sites of interest, such as chalk white horses on the hillside, while still embracing the best of the modern world, too.

Throughout, the books offer a wide range of characters, making their way through life, creating a few mistakes along the way, but ultimately discovering how to set their minds to achieve the very things that they truly want in life.

The Well-Travelled Book is quite a special and unique series of books well worth checking out on Amazon.

I hope you have enjoyed reading this book. Please leave a review on Amazon and tell other people about this book, thank you.

For a full list of books by

Tony Brassington

Please visit his website

www.tonybrassington.co.uk

or

Amazon

Tony Brassington

Made in the USA
Monee, IL
28 May 2021

69674952R00053